First published by Parragon in 2012

Parragon
Queen Street House
4 Queen Street
Bath BA1 1HE, UK
www.parragon.com

ISBN 978-1-4454-8776-2

Printed in Poland

Disney Princess

Tangled Ever After

Bath • New York • Singapore • Hong Kong • Cologne • Delhi
Melbourne • Amsterdam • Johannesburg • Auckland • Shenzhen

Spring had sprung, and Flynn had a surprise for Rapunzel. They took a walk through the forest.

Flynn wanted to be alone with Rapunzel, but Max wanted to keep guard and Pascal went along to play.

Finally, evening came, and Flynn took his chance to jump into a boat with Rapunzel. The lovely night reminded them of when they first watched the floating lanterns together.

Flynn put his hand in his pocket – he was going to propose! But oops, he did need Pascal and Max after all, because they had the ring!

"Will you marry me?" Flynn finally asked.

"Yes!" Rapunzel replied happily.

On their way home,
Rapunzel wanted to tell
everyone their news!

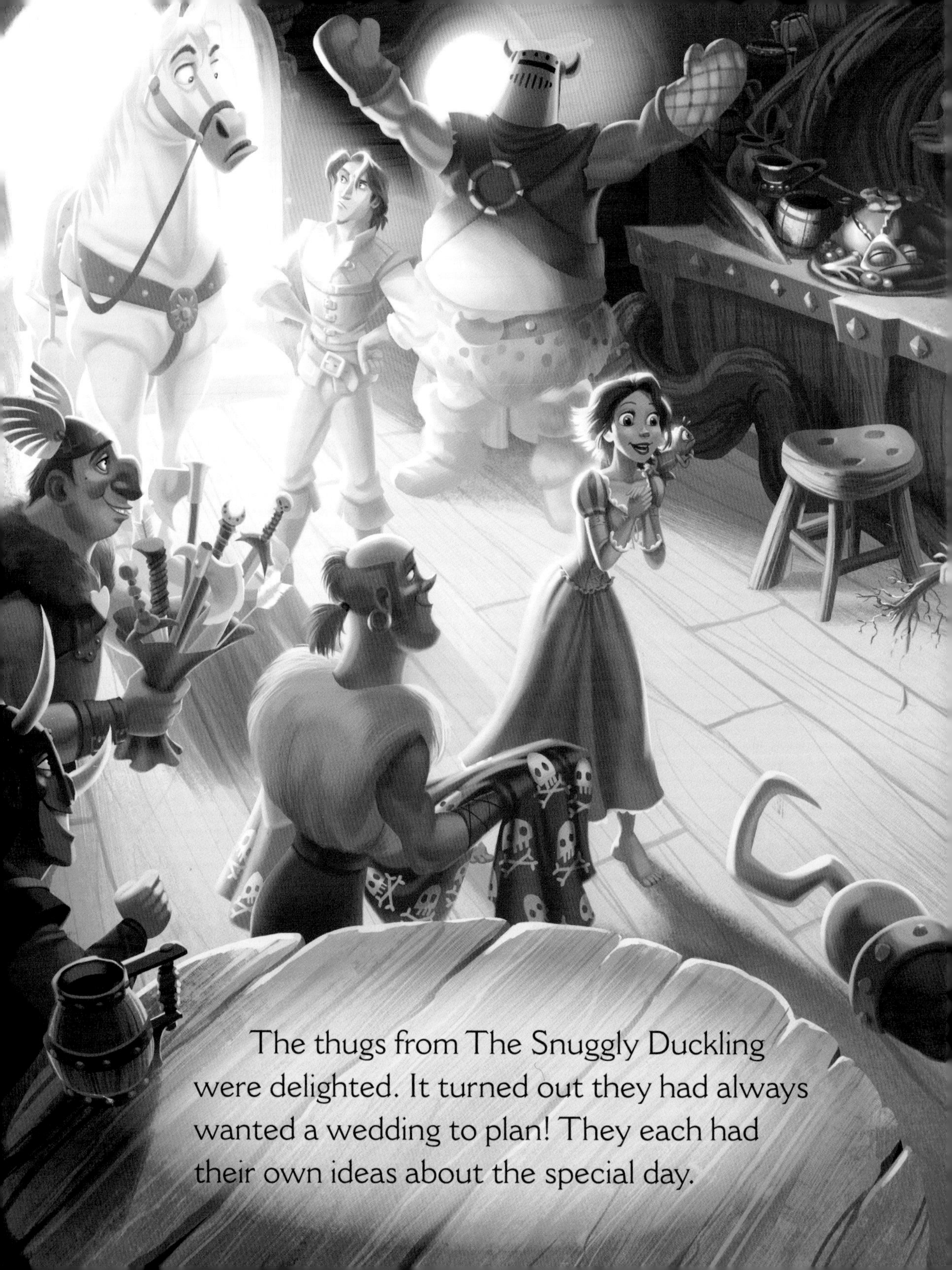

The thugs from The Snuggly Duckling were delighted. It turned out they had always wanted a wedding to plan! They each had their own ideas about the special day.

One of them, Attila, helped Rapunzel to design a cake.

They baked and iced, but nothing seemed quite right.

But finally, they created the wedding cake of Rapunzel's dreams!

Next, Tor helped Rapunzel choose the flowers.

Rapunzel chose some wild flowers from a field.

As for who would carry the rings – the choice was easy! Maximus and Pascal were very proud to accept.

When it was time to find a wedding dress, Rapunzel wanted to design her own. She drew lots of pictures . . . but simply could not make up her mind!

The pub thugs tried to help, but their dresses didn't seem right either.

Luckily, the Queen arrived. "Darling," she said. "I want to help you find the perfect dress."

And she did . . .

On the morning of the wedding, bells rang throughout the kingdom. Everyone was excited to see the King and Queen riding happily in the royal coach.

Max and Pascal were excited too – that is, until Max sneezed, and the rings flew into the air!

As Max and Pascal chased after the rings, the King proudly took Rapunzel's arm.

Flynn was so happy when he saw Rapunzel in her beautiful dress.

Luckily, nobody had any idea what Max and Pascal were up to . . .

Max and Pascal were racing through the kingdom after the rings! They were causing a lot of chaos.

Max ran straight through some drying clothes as he chased one ring . . .

. . . and Pascal chased the other ring into the air.

They finally caught the runaway rings . . . but then they crashed right into the tar factory!

Max and Pascal quickly left the factory and raced to the wedding. They arrived just in time!

Even though their ring-bearers now looked a bit strange, Flynn and Rapunzel were glad they were there.

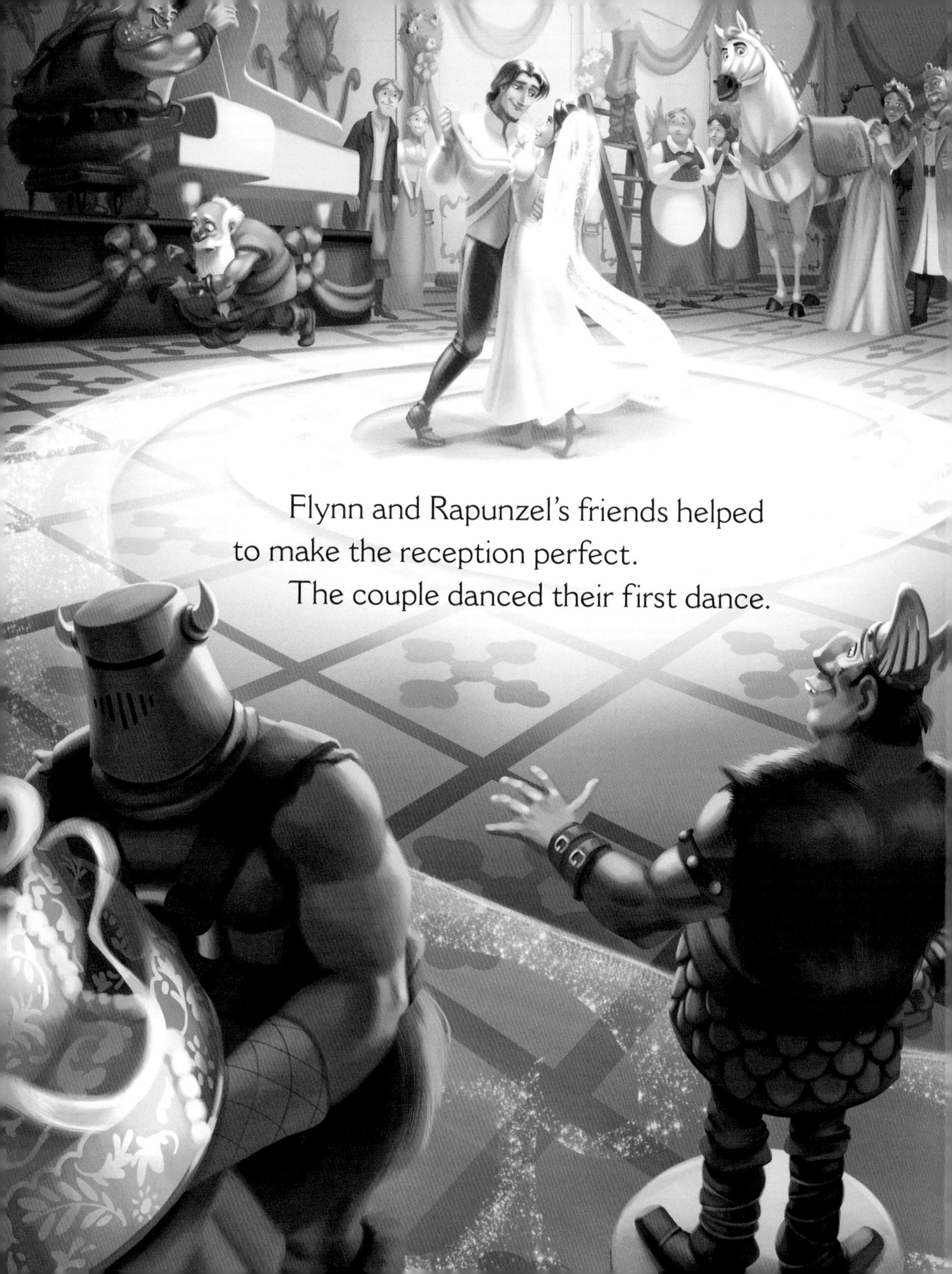

Flynn and Rapunzel's friends helped to make the reception perfect.

The couple danced their first dance.

They cut the wedding cake and were the first to taste it. It was delicious!

JUST
MARRIED

And as the newly married couple rode away in their wedding coach, Rapunzel cried out happily . . .

"Best. Day. Ever!"